For grandparents who live far away and grandkids who don't always want to play.

To my daughter who I love and my family who I cherish.

www.mascotbooks.com

I Wish I Wish I Was a Fish

For more information, please contact:
Mascot Books
620 Herndon Parkway #320
Herndon, VA 20170
info@mascotbooks.com

Library of Congress Control Number: 2020901234

CPSIA Code: PRT0320A
ISBN-13: 978-1-64307-568-6

Printed in the United States

I wish
I wish

I was
a fish.

My name is Kinley and I bet you wonder why I would wish such a wish. Well take a seat, and listen up, because it all started with this. . .

I waited in my room for another afternoon where Grandma and Grandpa would soon come to swoon.
I know they'd arrive pinching my cheeks and kissing my head, forcefully giving hugs and snugs and probably smells of old rugs.

As I waited in my room planning my escape from another boring grandparent playdate, I noticed a fish bowl that wasn't there before.

I asked Mom and I asked Dad if they were the ones who had given me this pet. My dad said it was Mom and Mom bet it was Dad. All I know is that it is totally RAD!

I ran back to my room to check the fish out. He floundered and flopped and fished about. I had never seen a fish like this before—twinkling, glowing, and shimmering gold.

I poked at the glass and tried to give it a kiss, but the glass kept me away. I suddenly was struck with the idea for a pretty witty wish.

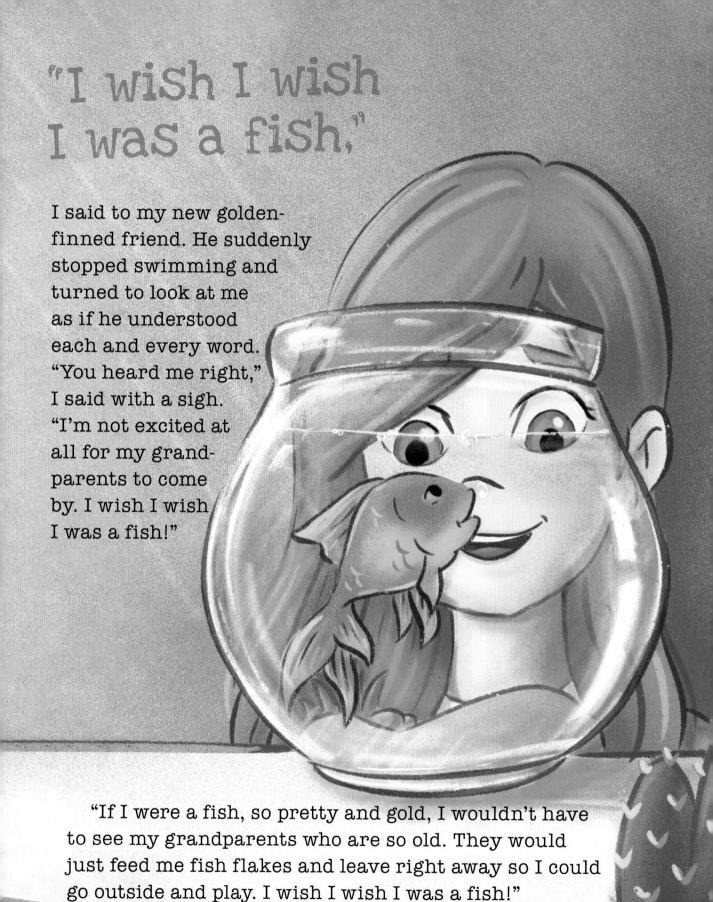

"I wish I wish I was a fish,"

I said to my new golden-finned friend. He suddenly stopped swimming and turned to look at me as if he understood each and every word. "You heard me right," I said with a sigh. "I'm not excited at all for my grandparents to come by. I wish I wish I was a fish!"

"If I were a fish, so pretty and gold, I wouldn't have to see my grandparents who are so old. They would just feed me fish flakes and leave right away so I could go outside and play. I wish I wish I was a fish!"

Suddenly the room began to spin. I felt a wet fin and a splash of water. The room spun about harder and harder!

When the room stopped spinning, I could not see straight. I tried to walk but, to my surprise, it felt like I was floating in clear blue skies.

I went to my left and I went to my right and tried to walk forward with all my might. I was transformed into the bowl of water inside my room, and oh thank goodness, not a moment too soon!

The doorbell rang and my grandparents arrived. Mom called up to me once, twice, three times, but when I tried to call back, bubbles just floated out of my little fish mouth, not a sound attached.

I did it, I did it! I thought to myself with glee. *And the best part is no one will even know it's me! My wish came true and I can just fish about!*

I did a quick spin and blew some bubbles. I wouldn't have to play or hug or kiss or snuggle! I could just float about eating my fish snacks and no one would bother me and that was that!

My grandparents came into my room looking high and low. Dad stepped in behind them with a puzzled look and said, "Where did she go?"

My grandma and grandpa arrived with excited smiles, but now everyone looked around concerned, wondering where was that child?

"Kinley?" they shouted, leaving my room in a hurry. I began to wonder if I was making them worried.

They rushed past my door one way, then back the other. Dad seemed confused, his words all in a stutter. "She was just here. . .I know she was home. Where could she be? Where did she roam?"

I heard Mom grab her phone quick and, with three little motions, her phone went

click, click, click.

She frantically described my red hair and blue eyes. She told someone on the phone I was just about three-foot-five.

She said, "Kinley was just here," but they only replied, "Ma'am there is nothing we can do—not until she's been gone for a day or two!"

Mom hung up the phone and sat down and sighed. "We lost our little girl," she said, letting out a big, sad cry.

I felt a weird feeling as I watched from my corner. My little fish reflection bounced back from the bowl. "I wish I wish I was me again," I said softly, thinking this might be causing some trouble.

I have to let them know I'm here! I thought. I swam in circles trying to show I was there. *Why did I wish this silly wish*, I thought to myself.

Grandma and Grandpa waited in my room. Grandma sat silent and Grandpa paced to and fro. He noticed me in the corner inside of my fish bowl.

He paced over to take a good look at me. He dropped in some fish flakes but then went right back to looking out the window to see if he could spot his missing granddaughter that he came to see.

Nothing happened. I was still a fish with golden fins and little fish lips. My grandpa told Grandma, "Now we must go. It's getting late and we have to help find Kinley, you know."

I heard the front door close as my grandparents left. They only came once or twice a year because they had to fly from far away to get here. It could be a long time before they get to come back.

I sank to the bottom of my tank from the top. I landed on a rock feeling so low that I couldn't even flop. "I wish I wish I was me again," I said with a little fish cry. But nothing happened again as I laid on my side.

My room was now dark and empty, but I heard the front door once again. Quickly Grandma and Grandpa poked their heads back in.

"We forgot to mention the fish we had bought. We saw it in her room in a lovely little spot. We brought some special food to keep her new pet in a great mood."

Grandma and Grandpa came into my room to leave the rest of my present. With tears in their eyes, they set down the food—they weren't mad at me, but sad to my surprise.

They sat down on my bed looking confused. "Where ever could she be?" Grandma said sad and blue. Grandpa hugged her tight and said, "I'm sorry. I know you were looking forward to this since forever and we had to cancel last time due to the weather."

I watched helplessly from my bowl in the corner thinking how badly I wished this were over. *How could I be so selfish when my grandparents come over?*

I closed my fish eyes and blubbered out of my fish mouth,

"I WISH I WISH I WAS ME AGAIN!"

The room spun and I flew about, feeling weird and dizzy. I closed my eyes so tight, wishing with all my might to hug my grandparents and make things right!

"KINLEY?!" I heard as I opened one eye. I was dripping wet, not an inch of me dry! Grandma and Grandpa moved like a flash, grabbing me up before a single second passed.

I reached out and hugged back
with both my arms so tight,
thankful to hug and snug them
and relieve their fright.

"Mom! Dad!" I yelled so loud,
they came barreling in confused
and proud. To their delight,
and mine, they saw me back in
my room hugging Grandpa and
Grandma not a moment too soon.

They didn't care where I'd been or why I was all wet since everyone was so happy to see me, I'm willing to bet.

I now know for certain that my grandparents miss me every second they are gone and they can't always fly from far away to come and play.

I hugged them so tight and gave them a kiss and wished for a much much better wish.

"I wish I could see you every day and that we could hug and snug and play. I'm sorry I wasn't here to let you swoon. I promise never again to miss grandparents' playdate. The next one can't come too soon!"

That is my story about my silly wish to be a little fish. Now I call Grandma and Grandpa every chance I get to tell them about my little fish pet and wish them well and tell them I love them. I count down the days until they visit again and bring hugs and snugs and my favorite smell of old rugs!

About the Author

Beau Blakeman is a father of two who currently resides in Missouri with parents across the country. He was inspired by real life situations with his own kids to write a book to help bring everyone together and remind us of the importance of time with family. *I Wish I Wish I Was a Fish* is his first publication. He hopes to give grandparents a tool to break the ice with their grandkids who they may not get to see as often as they would like.